a HARE'S hair changes with them all.

With
love
to
PAUL
and
PHILIP

ANIMALS BORN ALIVE AND WELL

BY RUTH HELLER

House Mouse

Publishers • GROSSET & DUNLAP • New York

1983 PRINTING

MAMMALS
are
animals with fur or hair
who nurse their young
and breathe fresh air.

They don't lay eggs
except these two.
These are the only
two who do.

Spiny Anteater

They
don't
lay
eggs,
as
I have
said,
they're
born

alive and well
instead.

Duckbill Platypus

Sometimes a
MAMMAL'S
hair
is scant,
as
on
the
thick-
skinned
ELEPHANT.

African Elephants

Pekinese

Yorkshire Terrier

But here's a pair with hair,

Okapi

Zebra

Ring-tailed
Lemur

and
here
are
lots
with
stripes
and
spots.

Giraffe

Cloud
Leopard

Tiger

Leopard

Nine-banded
Armadillo

Three-banded
Armadillo

Pangolin

And these have scales and

Porcupine

spikes like nails...but all of them are MAMMALS.

So are
CAMELS,

and like all the others,
they are nourished
by
their
mothers.

Dromedaries

Gazelle

MAMMALS
wild
and...

Deer

Stoat

MAMMALS
tame

all do more or less the same.

When they are
very, very small
into their
mother's pouch
they crawl
and grow
just like this
KANGAROO.

MARSUPIALS
are different
but they are
MAMMALS,
too.

KOALAS
are
MARSUPIALS, too.

MAMMALS
all
breathe air,
you
understand.

*Bighorn
Sheep*

This
isn't
hard
for
those
on
land,
or
even
those
found...

Moose

Mandrill

Panda

Rhinoceros

Hare

Guinea Pig

Aardvark

Kangaroo Rat

Weasel

Squirrel

Fallow Deer

Wild Goat

Bison

Red Fox

Hippopotamus

Giant Anteater

Prairie Dog

underground...

Mole

Shrew Mole

or those who fly,

Bat

or climb up high.

Marmoset

Tarsier

Gibbon

Baboon

Sloth

Bush Baby

Gibbon

Spider
Monkey

But MAMMALS living in the sea

Porpoise

Sperm Whale

Walrus

Seal

have to surface frequently.

Sea Otter

Dolphin

Manatee

Narwhal

Porpoise

The
PORPOISE,
WHALE,
and
MANATEE
have their babies
in the sea.

Humpback Whale

Manatee

The
WALRUS,
SEAL,
and
OTTER
prefer to
leave the
water.

Otter

Walrus

Seal

Walrus

These
are
prehistoric
but
they were
MAMMALS,
too.

Gomphotherium

Glyptodont

Their names
are very
long indeed
and
may be
very hard
to read.

Baluchitherium

Macrauchenia

The
largest
MAMMAL
is
the
BLUE WHALE.

The
smallest
is
the
SHREW.

Shrew

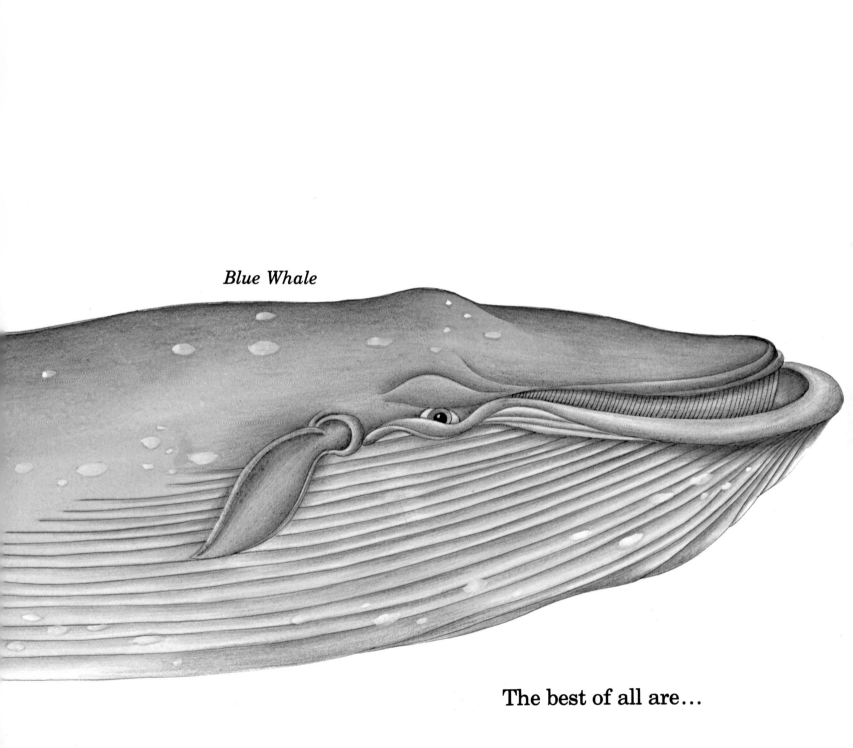

Blue Whale

The best of all are…

PEOPLE,
just like
me
or
you.

All of us are MAMMALS.

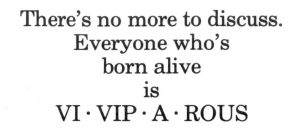

There's no more to discuss.
Everyone who's
born alive
is
VI · VIP · A · ROUS

Cheetah

Tapir

Hedgehog

Sheep

Horse

Pig

Snowshoe Hare